D1178311

D1133719

For Michele and Leon,
thank you both.

MYRIAD BOOKS LIMITED
35 Bishopsthorpe Road, London SE26 4PA

First published in 2003 by
PICCADILLY PRESS LIMITED
5 Castle Road, London NW1 8PR
www.piccadillypress.co.uk

Text and illustrations copyright
© Dana Kubick, 2003

ISBN 1 84746 118 2
EAN 9 781847 461186

Cover design by Fielding Design Ltd

Printed in China

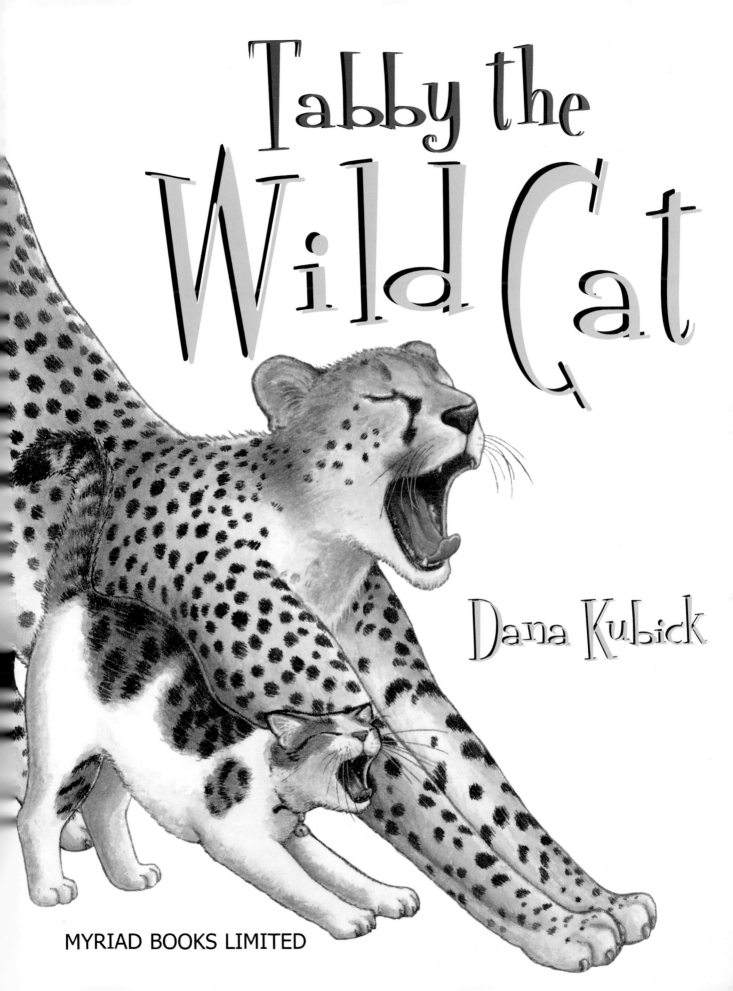

Tabby the Wild Cat

Dana Kubick

MYRIAD BOOKS LIMITED

When Tabby looks into the mirror
he doesn't see a small cat, he sees
himself as a big, brave, wild cat.

He doesn't see his home
as comfortable rooms,
but as a vast wilderness
full of adventure.

At night, Tabby dreams of hot sultry nights,
sleeping under the moon and stars.

When morning light comes, Tabby is the first one to wake.

He goes out to patrol his territory and to walk in the tall grass.

He climbs to the very
top of the garden shed

. . . to watch over
his kingdom.

It's time to explore.
With big jumps, he leaps
from cliff to cliff.

When he gets thirsty,
Tabby drinks from majestic lakes.

He stalks his prey with silent steps.

He pounces.

But when he gets hungry,
it is nice to know . . .

. . . there is someone to
look after him.